The Friendly Creeper Diaries: The Moon City

Book 6: The Moon Dragon

Mark Mulle

DEDICATION

This book is dedicated to all Minecraft lovers.

CONTENTS

DAY 11

For a full minute, I couldn't speak. All I could do was stare at the Moon Dragon. I had never seen such a creature before. I didn't even know that it was possible for something like this to exist. Sure, I had heard of the Ender Dragon. On top of that, David had told me a few times of legends where dragons were everywhere in the Over World.

But to see a jewel encrusted dragon in front of me was not the secret I was thinking they would be hiding. Star was looking at me as if she was afraid I was going to faint or something.

"Are you okay?" She finally asked me.

"This is what you guys are protecting...this dragon?"

Star nodded, "Yes. My people have remained down here in hiding to keep this dragon well hidden. It is extremely powerful. My people have a special connection to it. It listens only to us, you see, and if someone in the Over World were to try to control it...well, it wouldn't go well."

"This is what the kings want."

"Correct. They want to have the Moon Dragon for themselves. They want to wield its power and have it do their bidding. They would need one of us then too, of course, since it would only listen to someone with our powers."

"And what, Anderson is going to unleash this thing on the Over World?"

As if the Moon Dragon was bored of our conversation, it lowered its head back down to the ground. Its eyes closed and I could see rubies on its eyelids.

"Those jewels. How is that possible?"

"We don't know for sure. We know only the stories."

"Which are?"

Star tilted her head thoughtfully as she looked at the dragon, "My people used to say there were tons of these jewel dragons. See, the Sun City used to be on top of an active volcano. This was a long, long time ago, of course. The legend states there was a greedy king who wanted more than just his wealth and jewels. He wanted power."

"And?"

"He took all his wealth and went to the volcano and tossed the jewels into the lava. He had enchanted the jewels before he had tossed them in there. And so the magic hit the lava and it gave birth to these diamond dragons. Tons of jeweled dragons poured out of the volcano."

Star sat down on the steps leading towards the dragon, as if she was tired. I couldn't blame her. I sat down next to her even though I really didn't feel like getting close to that dragon.

"The dragons were powerful and threatened to overtake the Over World. My people worked together to reign them in. We discovered how they listened to us but we could also see how terrible they were. They were too strong. They could destroy anything if we told them too. Whatever the king did, he had created something awful. My people began to fight about what to do."

"Let me guess – some people wanted to rule with the Moon dragons and others wanted to protect them."

Star shot me a tired smile, "Exactly. Some people said we could use them to rule. We could be the strongest people on the planet. But other people disagreed. They said the powerful Moon dragons needed to be sealed away. They thought we needed to hide them until the final one passed away."

"So, what happened?"

"Civil war broke out. The legends say it was a great battle, a long war, that tore up the Over World. In the end, that's how the Sun City was created. They lost but refused to stay below and guard against people discovering the dragons. Eventually, they lost their magic."

"But your people stayed behind?"

"We stayed here, in the Moon City, and that is where we have remained. We are supposed to keep the Moon dragons away from the Over World. This is the final one."

"Do you still believe what you said earlier before Anderson did this – about how you guys could work with the king?"

"Yes," She said simply, "I think we have one dragon remaining. We could work with him and work something out. Maybe show the king how its power is too much for this world. Or maybe I'm just being selfish. I just want to be out of this dark, damp city and be where everyone else." She shrugged a little and looked down at her feet.

"Nothing wrong with that," I replied, trying to comfort her, "You know, I spent so long in my village. For a while, I didn't even think about what could be out there. It seemed so scary. But when I finally left…"

"It was amazing?"

"No, it was still scary," I said and Star laughed, "But it was also amazing. There is so much out there. Terrifying things but also fantastic things. I met people I never would have seen in my life. The world is a huge place. Wanting to get out of living underground is pretty understandable."

"Maybe I was wrong about the king ever accepting the Moon Dragon and not trying to use it for evil. Maybe I was putting myself first. But even so, it doesn't matter now. This entire time Anderson was planning on going into the Over World and taking the throne for himself."

"So, basically…we have to stop Anderson and we have to make sure the king doesn't try to use the Moon Dragon."

"That about sums it up, yes."

"Wonderful."

"Yeah, we are up against amazing odds." She stood up, brushing off some dirt on her knees and eyed the sleeping dragon.

"So, we got here first. What's the plan?" I asked, getting to my feet as well.

"Make sure we have it secured and wait until Grace arrives, I guess."

"Seems like...a bad plan."

Star laughed grimly, "Yeah, it isn't very good, is it?"

"Can we move it somewhere?"

"I mean, we could but this thing is massive. We'd alert anyone almost instantly."

"Yeah, good point. But leaving it here...we know Anderson is coming here. And if Grace moves too slowly, he'll be here with his skeleton army before they get here. Then what? No way we can fend them off ourselves."

Star bit her bottom lip nervously, "I don't know. Where would we take him?"

"There is a way to take him out of here, right?" I asked.

"Yeah," She pointed over to a wide tunnel on the opposite side, "Once a month, they take him out there so he can stretch his wings."

"So, we take him out that way."

"Yeah, but then what? Anderson will follow us."

"So, we take him to where Anderson can't follow, right?"

Star knew it was a crazy idea. But it was also a bad idea to stay here like a sitting duck and wait for Anderson to show up. We couldn't just let him waltz in here and take the Moon Dragon. We had to do something.

"I've never flown on his back before. Only the council has."

"Yeah, but you were smart enough to follow them to see what the secret was," A thought struck me, "Wait, so only the council knows about the Moon Dragon?"

She nodded, "That's right. The rest of us aren't told because I guess the council is afraid someone would try to take the Moon Dragon for themselves. We think they (council) are hiding something that would let the Over World know about the dragons, not an actual dragon. The people of Moon City except of the Council think all the Moon Dragons have all died."

"Well, great idea. Anderson is after it and the rest of the city has no idea it exists. We have to hurry up."

Star exhaled slowly and nodded. She was nervous but how could she not be? We were basically going to go over to a dragon and try to ride him.

The dragon seemed to sense her walking over because he opened his eyes. Funny how a few minutes ago, we had both been calling the dragon an 'it' but now we were calling the dragon 'him'.

"Please don't eat me," Star said to him, "Please, I really don't want to be eaten. I'm trying to help you."

She held out her hand towards the Moon Dragon. Even though I knew that the Moon Dragons were supposed to listen to her people, I was still nervous. Star wasn't part of the council. Would the Moon Dragon still listen to her?

The Moon Dragon moved his head over to her hand. In the torchlight, the flames bounced off of the jewels and made the entire dragon look as if it was sparkling. There was a large jewel in the middle of his head. It looked like a diamond. Star took a deep breath and placed her hand against the diamond.

Instantly it lit up and began to glow. The Moon Dragon lowered himself flat down to the ground and moved his wings so that Star could climb on his back. She exhaled and looked over at me, motioning for me to come over.

I hurried over although this was really the last thing that I wanted to do in the entire world. The idea of going on this dragon's back and flying who knows where did not fill me with joy. But I knew we couldn't wait around for Anderson to show up.

Star climbed onto his back and tried to wrap her arms around his neck. I got to the dragon and he suddenly turned his head and glared at me. I stopped in my tracks.

"Uh, I don't think he wants me on him."

Star closed her eyes and flattened her hands against his neck. It looked as if she was communicating with him. Her skin was even glowing. I didn't move. If she wanted to talk to the Moon Dragon and convince him not to eat me, I wouldn't stop her.

Then the dragon relaxed a little and turned his head away from me.

"Okay, hurry up." She said.

I was about to hop on the dragon but before I could do that or ask what Star had done to make the creature relax, the doors to the room opened. I looked over my shoulder to see Anderson stalking into the room.

When he saw us, he glared. Skeletons were following him in. Star grabbed one of my arms and began to yank me onto the Moon Dragon.

"Gotta go!" She exclaimed.

"Stop them!" Anderson cried.

Star mumbled something to the dragon and then he got to his feet. The ground shook underneath even if it were just small steps.

"Get them and do not injure the dragon!" Anderson yelled.

Skeleton archers ran up, crouching and aiming their golden bows at us. Star was mumbling at the dragon so quietly that I had no idea how he could hear her. But somehow, perhaps through their connections, he was. The dragon turned towards the tunnel and then he outstretched his wings.

I had read about dragons and see drawings of them over the years. But I had never seen a Moon Dragon's wings. They were massive and inlaid with glittering diamonds, rubies and sapphires. They looked as if they were on fire from the way the torchlight hit them.

The wings were so large that it knocked the skeleton archers off of their feet. Then he turned around to face the tunnel as Anderson was screaming behind us. I held onto Star and wanted to close my eyes.

But even though I was scared, I didn't close them. Instead, I watched as the dragon flapped his wings. The breeze from the wings fluttering made Anderson stumble. Then the Moon Dragon lifted off of the ground.

It was entering the tunnel now. The tunnel was dark and I couldn't see anything. The room behind us grew smaller and smaller as the dragon took us down it. He began to pick up speed as the tunnel grew wider.

Then I could see the end of the tunnel. All I could see on the other side were dark shapes but it was a bit lighter. I dug my hands into Star's sides as the Moon Dragon burst from the tunnel.

Below us was nothing but darkness. I tried not to look down and instead focused on the area ahead of us. The city had crumpled into ruin from this angle, as if part of it had sunken completely into the dark hole. Maybe it had been like that from fighting. In any case, the dragon flapped his giant wings and rose up higher.

"Now what?" I yelled in Star's ear as she gripped the dragon.

I looked behind me to see what was going on in the remains of the Moon City. The skeletons had spread out across the city. I could see pockets of fighting. David was down there somewhere. I just hoped that he was okay.

The Moon Dragon was circling the empty space below us as if waiting for Star to tell him what to do.

"I have an idea but it is sort of terrible!" She called to me.

"Do it anyway! Or else the skeletons will peck us off!"

She nodded and then leaned forward to the dragon. The Moon Dragon brought his head back and let out a mighty roar. I cringed. It was so loud. I had never heard anything like it in my life. Being on his back, up this high, as he roared angrily was incredibly scary.

Then he took off like a shot. He was going up, up, up, to the roof of the cave. I was suddenly regretting telling Star to do her crazy plan. Were we just going to crash through the top of the cave?

At the last possible second, the Moon Dragon tilted downwards. We were gliding across the top of the cave. We were too high up for the skeletons to get us. As we crossed the large hole at the edge of the city, I tried to see where we were going.

There was nothing for a minute or so. The only thing was the Moon City growing smaller behind us and the darkness below us. Then I saw it. If the Moon City looked ruined, the things in front of us looked downright destroyed. They looked like ruins even older than the city itself.

The Moon Dragon swept us over a broken down looking cluster of buildings and then sank to the ground. Star slipped off of him and landed on the ground. She turned around and held out her hand to me.

I grabbed it and hopped off of the dragon. He looked content now. His head was raised and he was looking around almost happily at wherever we were.

"What is this place?"

"In our civil war, this section of the city was completely destroyed. Half of it sunk into the depths. This is the old city. Just ruins. But they won't have a way to get over here. It gives us more time to figure things out."

"So the dragon is hidden but we are stuck here."

"For now, yes. Grace will need help – all the help."

"Yeah but Anderson is going to want to come over here to get to the dragon. Even if he hid, it is still risky. Feels as if we are back at square one again," I sighed and looked around, "Good thinking though. This place is a lot harder to get to."

Star looked pleased, "Thanks. I've never actually been over here before."

Amazingly, the dragon had fallen asleep. So he was a bit lazy. I guessed being the most powerful creature alive could make anyone tired. All around us were ruined buildings. They were in disrepair and made out of some substance I had never seen before. Ahead of us was what was probably a road at some point. Now, however, it was just covered in debris.

Star had gone over to the edge of the ruins and looked down into the darkness. She looked thoughtful.

"Any ideas?"

"Might have one although it would require a lot of magic use. Would probably tap me out again."

I went over to her, "What is it?"

She shook her head, "Get some rest first. Let me think it through before I tell you."

As much as I hated the idea of getting rest, I understood where Star was coming from. There was a battle going on in the city but ultimately we had to prevent Anderson from getting to the Moon Dragon. Since the two of us were tasked with watching the dragon, we needed all the rest we could get.

Even so, I still sat down and wrote everything in this journal. It took ages but I did it. I took some breaks though. Napped a lot while Star took watch.

It is my turn to keep watch again while Star naps. Then she wants to discuss her plan. I hope it is a good one otherwise we are going to be stuck over here while David and Grace are trying to keep Anderson down.

DAY 12

Finally, Star seemed to have mentally mapped out her plan. She came over to me as I slept near the dragon. I had relaxed enough to realize I wasn't in danger of it trying to bite me. Honestly, he seemed a bit lazy. I guess I couldn't blame him though.

"Want to hear my idea?" She asked me as I woke up and I nodded, "Alright. So, currently Anderson is the main bad guy, right? He's launching this attack and knows we are over here. He's going to try to get over here and we have to stop him."

"Right…" I said slowly, not sure where this was going.

"So the king would be the lesser of the two bad guys."

"You want us to take the dragon to the king?"

"I still think that my original plan stands. We can talk to him and convince him that this dragon is too powerful to be used in combat. In any case, we will protect the dragon from Anderson and we know for a fact he wants to use the Moon Dragon for his plan."

"This dragon have a name or something?" I asked, looking over at it.

"No. We don't name them. We aren't supposed to get attached."

"Well, he did save our lives." I pointed out.

Star looked thoughtful, "True. What should we name him?"

"What about Diamond? Because of the…" I motioned to his head.

"The big diamond in his head. Clever," She joked, "But sure, it'll work."

"So you want to take Diamond here to the king in hope that he won't go against us? That he won't take Diamond and just ruin the entire Moon City?"

"When you word it like that, it sounds like a terrible plan." Star replied.

"Lots of different things could happen. The king could just take Diamond for example. Unless there is something you aren't telling me?"

Star looked guilty almost instantly. I crossed my arms, wondering just what in the world she wasn't telling me.

"I can't tell you," She said quickly, "Because you're staying behind."

"What?" I exclaimed, alarmed, "I'm not staying behind."

"You have to, Mike. My plan hinges on me meeting with someone in the castle. We have someone undercover."

"Your people have a spy in the castle?" My eyes widened.

"Yes, that's right. He's sort of a back-up plan. That's all I can tell you. Technically, the council is the only one who is supposed to ever reach out to him but I'm going to. I'm going to tell him we have to talk to the king and tell him my plan."

"So, why do I have to stay behind?"

"Because while I am talking to him and the king, you have to help Grace and David down here. You have to stop Anderson from getting to the castle, or the king. You have to give me enough time to finish what I need to do."

I didn't like this plan. I didn't know what Star was planning. Who was the spy in the castle? What if he couldn't get through to the king? Or what if we managed to take care of Anderson but then the king took Diamond for himself?

But Star was looking at me confidently. She had a plan and if I had to stop Anderson from getting to her, then I would go along with it.

This was her city, after all, and her people. Diamond was technically her dragon.

"Fine," I relented, "I'll stay behind. You go to the king and see what you can do."

"The king hasn't interacted with anyone who wasn't on the council. My people are harsh and resistant to change. That could be why the king hasn't been too kind towards us. If I can convince him to work together..."

"And if you can't?"

"I don't know, Mike, one bad scenario at a time, okay? First, I have to get you back over there." She pointed to the rest of the Moon City.

"Can't you just drop me off? With Diamond?"

"No. See, I have an idea."

"But I won't like this either, will I?"

"No," She grinned, "Might be fun though."

Later that day

I stood at the edge of the ruins and glanced behind me. Star was hopping up on Diamond who yawned loudly. Honestly, he was more like a big dog than a dragon. She held onto him and looked over at me.

"Are you ready?"

"No, but let's do this." I replied.

"Alright, so, when Diamond and I take off, you are too. Run straight across the gap. Don't stop. Don't panic. Don't worry about skeletons shooting arrows at you. Just straight across. With you running across the gap, and me taking off with Diamond, Anderson's forces won't know who to focus on."

"And I'll be okay, right?"

"As long as my magic holds." Star replied.

"That isn't really comforting. What if your magic goes out in the middle of the giant hole?"

Star shook her head, "It won't. Near the end though, maybe…so run really fast, alright?"

I grumbled and tried to shove my fear down. In front of me was nothing but darkness. In the distance was the Moon City, which was where I needed to get. Star wouldn't let me drop down into the darkness. I had this.

I could feel a hum of energy off of Star and then a purple bubble appeared around me. I could see through it although everything was tinted purple. This was to keep all the arrows from actually striking me.

"Ready?" Star called out and when I nodded, she said, "Run!"

I took off like a shot. I ran straight ahead like she had told me to earlier. With Star's magic, she was basically creating a pathway for me to run towards the city. Above me, I could see a shadow across the purple as Diamond took the sky.

Between me running full speed across open air and the sudden appearance of Diamond, the skeletons began to open fire right away. Some tried to get me and others tried to shoot arrows with ropes towards Diamond in an attempt to bring him down to the surface again.

I was halfway across the pit now. Diamond was going to the top of the cave. Star was using magic to move the stones so they could break through the surface. A dragon breaking through the floor of the Sun City was going to get noticed. But Star said she had wanted it to be a big splash when she entered the city.

She was using a lot of magic. She was keeping me protected, keeping a pathway up for me and on top of that was trying to shift stone so they could smash through it easily. It was risky. At any point, she could sap her energy out. That would be serious trouble for me.

The skeletons had no idea what to do. They couldn't hit me and couldn't seem to stop Diamond. I was nearing the ledge now. We had crafted weapons as we had come up with the plan. I pulled out my sword as I came closer to the edge. Two skeletons were running to the edge to meet me there. As soon as I touched the ledge, Star's magic was going to cut.

I was almost there – just a few more steps – when suddenly the purple faded from my vision. I was vulnerable. Star's magic must be fading. I pushed myself forward and then I felt the invisible pathway that she had made suddenly disappear.

I was falling. I was falling quickly. I looked up and could see Star yelling at me but her words were lost on the wind. The stones in the roof were vanishing. In a few seconds, she was going to be gone.

I fumbled in my pack for my pickaxe. I had tied a rope to it to make a climbing rope out of it in case I needed it later. I guess I needed it now. Trying not to let the panic overtake me, I swung the pickaxe.

It was a good throw. It slammed into the stone and stuck. Clutching the rope, I closed my eyes and braced for impact as I landed against the stone. The wind was knocked out of me. Man, I didn't like climbing.

Above me, the skeletons were focused on me. Since Diamond and Star had vanished into the Sun City, they had turned their attention to me. Since the end of the plan had failed, I had to climb up quickly and hope the skeletons missed me with their shots.

One of the arrows dinged off my helmet and made me feel dizzy. Even so, I pushed it to the side and climbed up as quickly as I could. Another arrow bounced off my shield. Alright, so they were better at shooting than I had been expecting. I pulled myself forward.

My fingers were near the ledge now. As long as I didn't lose my grip, I could pull myself over. I had to move quickly though because the skeletons were going to be on me as soon as I got over.

I yanked the pickaxe out of the wall and then heaved myself over the ledge. A skeleton had been waiting for me and brought down its sword. In the dim light, I could see the flash of gold. Good. Weak equipment. I rolled at the last second and the sword smashed against the stone.

It snapped it half. The skeleton looked at the sword. If it had a face, it would have looked surprised. I was still on my back but I kicked my legs forward. The skeleton went toppling over the edge.

I kept my shield in front of me as I ran forward. The skeleton archers turned their bows to me, trying to take me down. I dodged two shots and then rolled underneath one of the skeleton's legs, swinging my sword. It turned to ash.

An arrow bounced off my shield. More skeletons were coming. I had to get out of here or I was going to be pinned down. The plan was to get to Grace and David to offer them assistance. I wasn't sure where in the city they were but they had to be noticing the influx of skeletons in this area.

Last time I had been pinned down, Star had been there with her magic to ward them. There was none of that this time. I had to rely on my own skills.

From my back, I pulled my bow forward. I had been able to craft one. It wasn't as nice as the bow I had from home but it would do. The Moon City was weak and crumbling. A correct arrow shot could bring buildings down.

There was a cluster of skeleton archers in front of me. They were on top of a building. The building didn't look very safe. There were wooden beams holding the entire thing up. If I could bring them down...

Even though I knew the skeletons were closing in around me, I tried to block them out. Bringing down this building would take care of most of them. The building falling down would distract the rest. All I had to do was shoot the arrow well enough to crack the two wooden beams.

Even from here, I could tell the two beams were already cracked. They were barely holding together. If there weren't already cracked, then it would have been a long shot but…

I let the first arrow fly. It slammed into the wooden beam. Even from here I could hear a cracking noise but it didn't collapse. A group of skeletons with swords were hurrying over to me. Time seemed to slow down. I focused on the shots.

I sent a second arrow into the air. The shot was clear. I was a lot better shooting at objects when they weren't moving. The arrow struck the wooden support beam and it cracked loudly. I watched as it fell apart. The skeletons that were coming towards me stopped to turn around and try to see where the noise was coming from.

One of the skeleton archers lost his footing and toppled off the building. The entire building slanted to one side as I shot two arrows, one after another, into the second beam. This one was weaker than the first one. The beam crumbled.

The entire floor holding the skeletons up shuddered and collapsed. The noise was so loud that all the skeletons coming after me were distracted. I took off running, not bothering to waste any time fighting with them. I had taken out the bulk of the archers. All I needed now was to find Grace and David.

I ran into the city, trying to stay away from any skeletons that were hurrying over to see why the building had fallen.

"Find that boy!" A voice cried out and I realized it was Anderson.

I ducked behind a ruined building and stuck my head out, peering around the corner. I could see Anderson. He was pacing the street, shouting at the skeletons.

"I want a full on assault on the city! That girl took the Moon Dragon and I want it!"

As he screamed, I realized he had a group of people tied up and shoved in a corner. From here, I could see David. Somehow, these people were captured in the fight. I didn't see Grace among the captives.

David didn't see me. I had to figure out how to rescue them. If Anderson saw me, I would be outnumbered quickly and thrown in with the rest of them. I kept my back close to the edge of the building and turned the corner. If I could sneak around the back, I could untie them. Then together, we could strike.

As I slunk past a group of skeletons, I held my breath. Anderson wanted to keep the council because he wanted them to serve him. Not only that but he could use them to convince the king to give up the throne. I needed to get them out of there.

At one point, I tripped over a stone. The stone was kicked forward and landed at a skeleton's feet. The skeleton stopped walking and looked down at it curiously. I ducked behind a pillar that had crashed down to the ground and hoped it wouldn't come over.

Luckily, the skeletons weren't exactly smart. They were skeletons after all. It wasn't as if they were full of brains. It lost interest in the stone and I was managed to scamper by it.

I was at the back of the destroyed building where the captives were. There was one skeleton standing guard by them. Anderson was pacing the street, still yelling.

"This is ridiculous! What did I make you guys for?! I will handle it myself. Watch the council members!" He snapped to the skeleton that was standing guard.

Then I watched as he ran off down the street. I had no idea where he was going but I couldn't worry about it now. This was my chance. I crept up behind the skeleton that was standing guard and attacked him swiftly. The skeleton turned to ash.

David was startled and looked over. His eyes went wide at the sight of me.

"Mike!"

"Keep your voice down." I whispered as I started cutting the ropes holding the council members.

"Where is Star? How did the dragon get out of here? We saw it in the sky."

"She took it to the surface." I said.

Next to David, a council member went, "She what?"

"She took it to the surface," I repeated, "She's going to some guy in the castle."

"Must be Edward." Another council member said.

"Is he the spy you guys have in there?" I asked as they began to get to their feet.

"That's right. Even so, taking the Moon Dragon out of here – it is madness. Completely insane. How did Star even find the dragon?" The first council member exclaimed.

"Spears, stop," The member at the end of the line said, "Getting upset isn't going to solve anything."

"Anne is right," David spoke up, "First off, we need to get out of the streets. Then we can regroup and try to find Grace," He turned to me, "Their magic is blocked. I'm guessing Star got hers back because she pretty much vanished through the ceiling."

"Yeah. We can go over it later. Let's get out of here."

David picked up the skeleton's sword out of the ash pile. We cut through the building, going away from the skeletons that were walking the main hall. Behind me, Spears was still grumbling. Great, this guy was going to be a real annoyance.

"Taking the dragon – which she isn't even supposed to know about, mind you. On top of that, using magic to leave and take him to the Sun City which goes against everything we stand for."

"Spears!" Anne snapped, "Enough. Star did what we failed to do which was get the Moon Dragon away from Anderson. Anderson, who is, let me remind you, a council member who is currently trying to take the throne for himself."

Spears finally fell silent. Anne marched up next to me. She was younger than the rest of the council and had large green eyes. She pointed to a tower that had seemingly been snapped in half.

"There."

We followed her. The skeletons didn't seem to be interested in this part of the city. I noticed that I hadn't seen anyone else besides the council and asked where they were.

"Anderson has them all," David replied grimly, "As a council member, he knew where everyone in the city lived. He has them in the building we were in earlier."

"Wonderful. Keeps getting better."

"Why didn't Star take you to the surface?" He asked.

"Part distraction and partly that she didn't want me to know what was going on. She seemed secretive about this…Edward guy." I replied as we opened the door to the tower.

"As she should be," Spears snapped, "Edward has been working with the king for years now. He is our spy and makes sure we remain hidden. The fact she had taken the Moon Dragon and is going to him – it will blow his cover."

Anne rolled her eyes, "Edward knows the king well. Even with the information that he is a spy, the king will be more prone to listen to him than Star. That is why she is going to him. It is clear what her plan is. Why can't you see that?"

Spears fell silent and crossed his arms.

"So, she thinks the king will listen to Edward?" I asked.

Anne nodded, "Has to be it. Star isn't stupid. She's smart as a whip. Would probably end up on the council one day…if there even is one after this."

The other two council members were silent. Everyone looked tired. Even so, I knew that we had to get Grace.

"Our magic is blocked." Spears finally said.

"Yeah, something Anderson is doing to you guys. I don't know what. Star got past it after some time passed. She really had to push through it though."

"Grace went to save the rest of the city. But we were outnumbered. Once Anderson blocked our magic, it was all over." Anne said.

"We have to stop Anderson from getting to the king. If his skeleton army goes to the surface, then he could get to the Moon Dragon." Spears said urgently.

"If he can stop Star's magic, that means if he gets close enough, he can sever her connection to the Moon Dragon. Which means he could take control of it. Did she think of that?"

My throat went dry, "Uh, probably not."

"I'm good with a bow. I will come with you two," Anne said, "This tower holds weapons in a secret spot."

Spears looked around, "I should probably stay here. Guard the tower with these two." He gestured to the other two tired looking council members.

Everyone knew Spears just didn't want to fight. But I was fine with him staying behind.

Anne opened a hidden door in the floor and pulled out a box. Inside were swords, shields and bows. There were also small vials of murky looking liquid that she put in her robes.

"Concentrated magic." She explained even though I wasn't sure what that even meant.

She grabbed her bow and David dropped the gold sword from the skeleton and picked up a diamond sword. Then he gave me an extra diamond sword.

"I'll take this extra bow," He said, "It isn't good for you to use but I might be able to get some shots in."

I nodded and then looked at Anne, "Do you know where we are going?"

"Yes. I know the back ways around the city. We should get there in time. Spears, you have to be prepared. Once I get the rest of the villagers free, Grace and I will send them over here. You protect them, okay? All three of you."

Spears gulped, looking nervous, but nodded.

"No time to waste. We leave in twenty minutes, okay?" She said to us.

That gave me just enough time to write in here. I scribbled everything down as quickly as I could. Not even sure any of it is legible. Even so, it is down in this journal.

Now to head back into the city to get Grace and the rest of the people living here. I really hope Star is going okay.

DAY 13

We set off into the city. Anne led us since she knew exactly where we had to go. She led us through back alleyways and across ruined buildings. David and I were both glad that she was tagging along.

As we walked, Anne looked up at the ceiling, "Crashing into the Sun City with a Moon Dragon is risky. Edward can try to help her convince the king…or the king will be so upset that Edward is technically a spy that it won't work."

"Yeah, but the threat of Anderson is bigger than Edward. I think that is what Star is hoping he will think." I replied as I stumbled over a rock.

We fell silent again as we came close to the city square – well, what used to be the city square anyway. It had fallen into disrepair, just like everything else had down here. We could see them instantly. The rest of the people of the Moon City were in prisons that had been crudely constructed from crafting tables against one wall. The statue in the middle of the city square had been broken apart and there were giant stones all over the city square.

"The statue has been like that for ages," Anne said to us as if she knew what we were thinking, "Our people never replaced it as a reminder about what our civil war had done to the city."

"So…the city square always looks this bad?" David joked.

Skeletons were pacing the square, clearly on look-out. These guards had iron equipment which would make things a little trickier. I was slowly coming up with a plan. When Anne went to step forward, I grabbed her and pulled her back.

"If your magic gets cut off down there, you'll be useless. We still don't know how he is blocking it. David and I need to go down there. We don't have any magic to block."

Anne looked as if she didn't like this idea but she knew that I had a point too. She pulled her bow off her back and nodded.

"I can cover you guys." She said.

I nodded and looked back out at the villagers, "We have to figure out how their magic is being blocked. It has to be something in the air. Something they are breathing in. Anderson tested it out on Star and now that he knows it works, he'll want everyone to be blocked from using their magic."

David was studying the city square and pointed to a glowing orb near one of the cells. It was purple and emitting out some sort of fog.

"What is that? I bet that's it."

I squinted and saw a couple more orbs around the other cells. David had to be right. The orbs had to be letting out something to block the magic of the Moon People.

"Alright. Well. We all knew this was going to be dangerous," I remarked, "David and I are going to go down there and distract the skeletons. We will try to take care of as many as we can. Anne, do you think you can see if your arrows can make the orbs explode?"

She nodded, already notching an arrow in her bow. I looked over at David. He looked excited. Even now, with everything that had happened, this sort of adventure was still right up his alley.

"Ready?" I asked him.

"Let's do this."

We climbed down the ledge we had been hiding on to look at the skeletons. We wanted to draw them away from the cages so Anne could work on taking the orbs down with her arrows. I took a deep breath and glanced at David. He nodded again. I would serve as the distraction then while David would attack first.

I ran out into the city square, making as much noise as possible. I pretended that something was chasing me and I was panicked about it. I kept gesturing to something behind me to cause the skeletons to be a bit more confused.

The skeletons seemed surprised to see me – well, as much as skeletons can be surprised. Two of them began to run over to me as if they were going to drag me into the cells. Behind me, I could see David sneaking up to one of the distracted skeletons and turning it to ash very quickly.

I raised my shield and blocked a blow from one of the skeletons. The iron swords were a lot heavier than gold and my arm vibrated from the hit. Then I spun around and blocked another hit from the second skeleton.

An arrow went flying over my head. It soared cleanly through the air and slammed into one of the orbs. It didn't break. A large crack formed against the swirling, purple orb.

By now, the skeletons were all on alert. They were coming after both David and I. We were locked in battle. They hadn't yet noticed that Anne was trying to break the orbs apart. That was good. Each second we were able to distract them worked to our advantage.

I managed to take down two skeletons as more came spilling out of a house nearby. I could see David gulp at the sight of so many skeletons. How had Anderson created so many? It was crazy to me that he had been able to hide all these skeletons.

Anne sent another arrow flying through the air. The first orb shattered. The purple smoke inside of it floated up to the sky and then vanished.

"Keep trying your magic!" I cried out to the first prison full of people as I blocked another hit from a sword.

The people in that cell listened. I could see them trying to call down their magic. I hoped they could push through it. I also hoped that since the orb was destroyed, whatever was left in the air would fade quickly.

Now that the first orb was destroyed, the skeletons knew what was going on. They were looking for signs of the archer, trying to find Anne. But Anne wasn't on the ledge anymore. She must have moved to a safer place because I could see her arrows flying through the air to hit the second orb.

I stumbled and David managed to yank me to my feet before I hit the ground. Now that the skeletons understood what was going on, it had turned into chaos. A few skeletons were still trying to come after us but a bulk of the skeleton army was looking for Anne.

The second orb cracked apart and fell to pieces. At the same time, the group in the first cell suddenly broke free. As the villagers stumbled out of the cell, I could see flames and ice coming out of their fingertips. They had gotten their magic back.

After that, the chaos seemed to grow even crazier. Everything was a flurry of combat, of David and I trying to take down skeletons, of Anne breaking the final orbs and everyone getting their magic back.

The skeletons stood no chance. For the first time, I truly understood why he needed the magic of the Moon People blocked. They were incredibly powerful. They took down the skeletons in a matter of minutes and soon there were none left.

Finally, it was all taken care of. The skeletons were gone and no more seemed to be coming. We had rescued the villagers. Anne came down from the spot she had been firing her bow from and hurried over.

"Where is Grace?" She asked the group.

"Anderson has her," A young girl replied, "He's taking her to the surface."

I could tell Anne wasn't sure what to do. If she came with us to get Grace, the villagers would be stuck with Spears who didn't seem to know what he was doing.

"We'll go," I said to her, "You take everyone back to the tower."

Anne tried to protest but David shook his head, "You need to watch these people. We'll get Anderson, Grace, Star – everyone. Trust us."

"Fine," She said with a sigh and turned to the group, "Everyone, with me. We have a base set up on the other side of the city."

David and I watched the group leave. Then we took off towards the front of the city, knowing we had to get to Anderson before everything got worse.

DAY 14

"Do we have any plan at all?" I asked David as we hurried towards the entrance of the city.

"Uh, I'm going to say no." He replied, "I mean, I have no idea what the surface is going to be like at this point. Anderson took his army up there, along with Grace, and Star has the Moon Dragon up there. No telling what we are going to stumble into."

"As usual."

"As usual." David replied but then he grinned at me.

"How can you be having so much fun?" I asked, shaking my head.

He laughed, "Come on, Mike. Danger aside, we are really trying to save this entire community. It's just like before," He hits my shoulder playfully, "This is what we've been looking for."

"What you've been looking for." I protested.

David just raised his eyebrows at me but didn't say anything back. We were at the entrance that Anderson had taken to us before. Normally, it would have been sealed over with rocks. We would have needed magic to get out – which was something we had forgotten to consider.

But in a stroke of good luck, the blocks were removed. Either Anderson or Grace had left it like this. In either case, we were able to hurry up to the exit of the Moon City into the Sun City.

We were halfway up the stairs when we heard the fighting. Swords against swords, shields blocking sword blows, and the cries of men giving orders. Anderson had definitely unleashed his skeleton army onto the Over World.

We burst into the city streets. Where this area had once been abandoned, it was now full of soldiers and skeletons. No one noticed us when we entered the area. They are all too busy fighting.

"Mike, look!" David exclaimed and pointed.

I turned my head and saw what David was pointing to. On the top of the castle was Diamond. He was roaring loudly and his entire body was glowing from the light hitting the jewels.

"Anderson is going to try to get to Diamond to cut off Star's connection to him. We have to hurry up." I said, tugging David forward.

"You named the dragon?" He asked as we ran through the streets.

I didn't bother to explain. We were low on time as it was. As we ran into the center of the city, trying not to get run over by people trying to flee and the battle raging around us, I finally saw a flash of Anderson.

He was going up the castle steps. He was alight with color, shining a deep purple. It was then I realized what he was doing. Those orbs and the ability to block people's magic – it all fed directly to him.

But we had destroyed the orbs back in the Moon City. What could be making Anderson stronger?"

"Grace." I said under my breath, knowing I was right.

That was why he had brought Grace with him. He was blocking her magic and using it for himself. I yanked David forward again and we cut through the battle. One skeleton came after us but David took care of it easily as we ran up the steps to the castle.

Anderson was in front of us. I didn't see Grace. He must have her somewhere with an orb nearby. I turned back to David.

"We have to split up!"

35

"What? Have you lost your mind?" He protested.

"You have to find Grace! He has her somewhere with one of those orbs nearby. He's going to be too powerful if he is using her magic!"

David knew I was right. I could tell he didn't want to leave but he also knew we had to cut Anderson off from Grace's magic.

"Where could she be?" David called out to me as Anderson blew back three soldiers with a gust of wind from his fingertips.

"Has to be somewhere nearby! He wouldn't have had time to hide her far away because the skeletons entered the city with him!" I cried out over the roar of battle.

David nodded, wished me luck and then took off into the battle. I watched him leave where he was quickly swallowed up by the battle. I turned back to Anderson. He was cutting a clean line up to the castle. I wasn't sure how close he needed to be to sever Star's connection to the dragon but I didn't want to take any risks.

I took off at a run. Anderson hadn't seen me. If I timed it right, I could tackle him to the ground. All I needed to do was distract him enough until David found Grace. As I took off at a run towards Anderson, I realized I had made a mistake.

Anderson had seen me. He had just been pretending that he hadn't. He turned around quickly and stuck out his hand. It was like running directly into a wall. I smashed into it hard and landed down on the ground, out of breath.

"You and your friend have been a thorn in my side," Anderson snapped, "Forcing me to start my plan early because you just couldn't leave things along. I am too powerful for you to run up and tackle creeper boy. Don't be a fool."

I tried to get to my feet but something was keeping me stuck in place. Whatever Anderson was doing to me made it impossible for me to move. He was looking down at me now.

"Do you know why my people lose their magic after using it too much?" He asked me and didn't wait for me to reply, "It's a failsafe our bodies have. Our bodies run out of magic and then has to recover. But what if we didn't need to recover? What if the magic never stopped coming?"

"You're draining magic from the rest of the Moon City people to give yourself infinite magic!" I exclaimed.

Anderson laughed, "Grace is the strongest person on the council. I wanted her nearby as a back-up. You know, just in case you and your friend messed things up again. Which, judging by the three seconds I lost my magic, I could tell you have."

"The people of the Moon City are saved," I said, "And now I'm going to stop you from becoming king."

Anderson sneered, "You really think so, boy? Not too long ago, you and the rest of your creeper friends lived in the village away from all of this. You are messing around with things you could never hope to understand."

"I understand someone trying to take over a group of people," I snapped, "I understand you wanting to use the dragon for your own evil scheme. Star and I won't let you do that."

"You think because the girl has taken the dragon up to the top of the castle it will do anything? She must think she is so powerful to be on the Moon Dragon! But as soon as I get close to her, the dragon will be mine – and so will the throne!"

Anderson kept talking. I realized he really loved to hear himself talk. This was his moment, after all, wasn't it? He had planned and schemed for a long time to have all of this come together. Of course he was going to talk my ear off.

I didn't bother to struggle. His magic was too strong and was keeping me in place. Even so, I didn't mind too much. As long as I kept Anderson talking, it would slow him down and give David more time to find Grace.

But we got interrupted. Out of the castle burst two men. One was the king. The second was an old man that had to be Edward. His fingertips were glowing gold from magic. Anderson stopped speaking and turned around.

His eyes narrowed at the two men, "So, what? The girl told you Edward worked for us and you are content to let him stand by you?" He said towards the king, "You are weak. Always have been. Move aside and I won't destroy you."

"Star came to me," Edward spoke, "Told me of what was going on. The king and I both know you have to be stopped. Power is nice and can help a kingdom. But no one wants this." He gestured around him.

"Spare me!" Anderson cried out and blue light crackled at his fingers, "The king has wanted the dragon for himself for ages!"

"It's true. At one point, I did want the Moon Dragon for myself. But I can see now why it had to remained hidden – why all of you have spent years to protect it. Sad how a young girl can see the power that must be kept locked up while a leader cannot."

"You can't stop me. I am too strong now. Even if you have your magic, Edward, I will ruin you."

Then Anderson attacked. Lightning came out of his fingers and shot towards the two men. Edward raised his hands and a gold shield appeared in front of them, blocking the attack.

Since Anderson was focused on them, his power slipped on me. This allowed me to get to my feet. I ran forward and tackled him to the ground. He let out a grunt of surprise. Suddenly, I was lifted up into the air.

"I told you!" He snapped, "I am more powerful than you can ever –"

Then I was falling. I hit the ground with a thud and the wind was knocked out of me. Anderson was staring at his hands in shock. I knew instantly that David must have found Grace somehow.

He had been using so much magic that instantly he was drained. I could tell because I had seen the similar expression on Star's face before. He looked dazed, as if he had no idea where he was. He tried getting to his feet but stumbled forward.

"His magic is gone!" I shouted at Edward.

He didn't waste any time. He stepped forward and the gold light circled around Anderson as he fainted.

I could hardly believe it. We had stopped him.

DAY 15

It has taken a lot of time to catch up in this journal but I finally have done it. The last couple of days have been a flurry of activity. Anderson was arrested. David had found Grace stuck next to an orb in a destroyed inn.

Star had drained herself out from too much magic use and had to be sent to medical. I saw her the next day, propped up in bed, reading a book.

"Hey." I said to her as I sat down across from her.

David followed me into the room and gave her a wave, "Doing okay?"

"Tired, but okay. Grace was here earlier. She offered me a spot on the council."

"What did you say?" I asked curiously.

"I told her I think we should get rid of the council. Most of our people didn't even know about Diamond down in the depths of the city. Didn't feel right. We talked for a while and worked it out."

"So...no more council?" David said.

Star nodded, "That's right. Edward and I had managed to convince the king about the threat of Anderson. Once he saw the power of Diamond and what Anderson was trying to do, he agreed that it wasn't something he had any interest in. So, we've worked out a treaty. It's going to be signed in a few days."

"Does this mean you get to walk around the Over World now?" I asked hopefully.

A big grin broke out across Star's face, "That's right. No more hiding underground anymore. Thank you both for help. I can't thank you enough."

"Not a problem." David said but he was smiling.

He nudged me with his arm. I knew what he was thinking. We had just wrapped up another adventure. We had helped save the Moon City. We had helped stopped Anderson. We had made sure Star was okay.

"What happened to Diamond?" I asked suddenly.

"Ah, well…he's still linked to me. I have him hidden somewhere out in the Over World. My secret though."

"Hope I get to visit him sometime."

David looked at me as if I was crazy, "You want to visit a dragon?"

"He's more like a big dog." I protested.

Star laughed and then we were all laughing together. It felt good. David had been right – I had needed an adventure after all. As we left the med bay to the hallway, David looked at me.

"So…what next?"

ABOUT THE AUTHOR

Mark Mulle is a passionate Minecraft gamer who writes game guides, short stories, and novels about the Minecraft universe. He has been exploring, building, and fighting in the game ever since its launch, and he often uses in-game experiences for inspiration on creating the best fiction for fellow fans of the game. He works as a professional writer and splits his time between gaming, reading, and storytelling, three hobbies and lifelong passions that he attributes to a love of roleplaying, a pursuit of challenging new perspectives, and a visceral enjoyment the vast worlds that imagination has to offer. His favorite thing to do, after a long day of creating worlds both on and off the online gaming community, is to relax with his dog, Herobrine, and to unwind with a good book. His favorite authors include Stephen King, Richard A. Knaak, George R. R. Martin, and R. A. Salvatore, whose fantasy works he grew up reading or is currently reading. Just like in Minecraft, Mark always strives to level up, so to speak, so that he can improve his skills and continue to surprise his audience. He prefers to play massive multiplayer online games but often spends time in those games fighting monsters one on one and going solo against the toughest mobs and bosses he can manage to topple. In every game, his signature character build is a male who focuses mostly on crafting weapons and enchanting, and in every battle, he always brings a one hander sword and a shield with as much magical attributes as he can pour into them. Because he always plays alone, he likes to use his game guides to share all the secrets and knowledge he gains, and who know—he may have snuck some information into his fiction as well. Keep an eye out for his next book!

Author's Note: This short story is for your reading pleasure. The characters in this "Minecraft Adventure Series" such as Steve, Endermen or Herobrine...etc. are based on the Minecraft Game coming from Minecraft ®/TM & © 2009-2013 Mojang / Notch

CPSIA information can be obtained
at www.ICGtesting.com
Printed in the USA
LVOW13s1954220217
525093LV00010B/1124/P